Watching Whales

Watching Whales

JOHN F. WATERS

ILLUSTRATED WITH PHOTOGRAPHS

COBBLEHILL BOOKS

Dutton / New York

To Sandy and Dan

Library of Congress Cataloging-in-Publication Data
Waters, John F., date
Watching whales / John F. Waters.
p.   cm.   Includes index.
Summary: Discusses the natural life of whales and human
excursions in boats to watch them in their own habitat.
ISBN 0-525-65072-5
1. Whale watching—Juvenile literature.   [1. Whale
watching.   2. Whales.]   I. Title.
QL737.C4W325   1991
599.5—dc20   90-28719   CIP   AC

Published in the United States by Cobblehill Books,
an affiliate of Dutton Children's Books,
a division of Penguin Books USA Inc.

Designed by Mina Greenstein. Printed in Hong Kong
First Edition   10   9   8   7   6   5   4   3   2   1

Photographic credits: Captain Aaron Avellar, Provincetown, 4
(bottom), 5, 10, 11, 13, 15, 24, 31, 37; BIOS Brier Island
Ocean Study, 3; photographed by Gordon E. Caldwell, 35;
L. P. Madin, WHOI, 6; New Brunswick Department of
Tourism, 14, 21, 23; Nova Scotia Tourism and Culture, 22,
27, 32; Anne I. Rabushka, WHOI, *ii*, 2, 18, 25, 38;
T. W. Ransom, The Whale Museum, Friday Harbor, WA,
16; John F. Waters, 8, 9, 12, 17, 19, 28, 29, 30; Mike
Williamson, *vi*; Woods Hole Oceanographic Institution
(WHOI), 4 (top).

ACKNOWLEDGMENTS

I am grateful to the following persons and institutions for their wonderful help in the preparation of this book:

Lee Campbell, Woods Hole, Massachusetts; Cathy Murphy, Image Bank Coordinator, Tourism, Recreation & Heritage, New Brunswick; Gordon Caldwell, Photographer, *Cape Cod Times*; Vicki Haller, Public Relations, Vancouver Public Aquarium, Vancouver, British Columbia; Lori Taylor, Department of Tourism and Culture, Halifax, Nova Scotia; Beth Helstien, Development Officer, The Whale Museum, Friday Harbor, Washington; Center of Coastal Studies, Provincetown, Massachusetts; Mike Williamson, Mingan Island Cetacean Study, South Hamilton, Massachu-setts; Deborah Tobin, Brier Island Ocean Study, Westport, Nova Scotia; Nancy Green, Public Information Office, Woods Hole Oceanographic Institution; Janet Lavin, International Wildlife Coalition, North Falmouth, Massachusetts; Depoe Bay Chamber of Commerce, Depoe Bay, Oregon; Susan Peters and all the members of her class, Osterville Bay School, Osterville, Massachusetts; New England Aquarium, Boston, Massachusetts; Pacific Whale Foundation, Kihei, Maui, Hawaii.

And a very special thanks to Captain Al Avellar and Captain Aaron Avellar of the Dolphin Fleet of Provincetown, Massachusetts, for their great help. And, of course, a big thanks to all the marine mammals of Stellwagen Bank.

*T*HERE IS something exciting about giants. They almost seem to come alive in books, and most are such frightening creatures. There are ferocious dinosaurs, fairy-tale ogres, and one-eyed Cyclopes. All are huge in size. If it were possible to meet one of these giants close up, it would be terrifying.

Today, there are real live giants living in the oceans of the world. And despite one of them being the largest animal ever to live on earth, they are not frightening. The enormous blue whale, that grows to be 100 feet long and weighs 160 tons or more, is, for its size, a gentle animal.

Most people never have an opportunity to see such a marine giant in person. Some find it hard to believe that animals so enormous truly inhabit the vast seas. But giant air-breathing whales do exist, and in the past few years more and more people have made short ocean trips to see all kinds of whales.

People do so for several reasons. First, whales are such magnificent and graceful creatures they are fun to watch in their own environment. Also, because for years whalers slaughtered them and almost wiped out entire species, there are not many of the giant whales to see. And, compared to land animals, giant whales are a bit of a mystery, because they live in the vast, deep oceans. People like to watch whales because whales are special.

With this great love for whales and a tremendous curiosity about them, there is a thriving

Humpback whales

whale-watching business on both coasts of the United States and at various ports in Canada. One of the more popular sites for whale watching in the East is off the coast of Cape Cod in Massachusetts where each spring there is a strange annual meeting of humans and whales. Whales arrive at a place called Stellwagen Bank to feed on fish, with the most common being the sand lance. There are also schools of cod, flounder, and pollack. Because the bank is shallower than water around it, the area is rich with tiny plankton, and all kinds of marine animals feed on plankton. Stellwagen Bank is located 12 miles south of Gloucester, Massachusetts, and stretches south for 18 miles. Its southern end is but five miles from the tip of Cape Cod. Many of the whales that feed in the waters of the six-mile-wide bank are on their way north to the cold-water feeding grounds in the North Atlantic from Canada to Iceland. Whale-watch boats cruise out several times a day. People of all ages are eager for a trip to watch the whales feed.

About the Whales

If the whale watchers on the East Coast are fortunate they may see finback (fin) whales, minke whales, and humpbacks. And on very rare occasions watchers may get a glimpse of a right whale. A right whale sighting is a rarity because right whales were overkilled by whalers, and estimates put their worldwide numbers only in the hundreds, with less than 300 living in the North Atlantic.

The length of the North Atlantic right whale averages 50 feet, and it weighs 70 tons, though some may weigh as much as 100 tons. Right whales feed on microscopic plankton and need 800 pounds of plankton a day. Their winter calving ground is along the Georgia and Florida coast. When they migrate north, they do not stay

Right whale

ABOVE: *Minke whale*

BELOW: *Finback whale*

long at Cape Cod, as they are heading for the Bay of Fundy and Brown's Bank, their summer feeding ground.

Minke whales (pronounced MINK-ee) are small, averaging 20 to 30 feet in length. They are found in numbers in the cooler waters of the world. Minkes are loners; therefore, they are seldom seen and when there is a Cape Cod sighting it is usually just a single whale. In contrast, the fin whale that is spotted is much larger, reaching lengths of 60 to 88 feet and weighing up to 50 tons. Finbacks calve in warm waters in the deep ocean and seldom concentrate in large numbers. They are usually seen off Cape Cod as they travel in groups of two to fifteen.

The humpback whales are the most numerous of all the whales seen off Cape Cod. About 100 spend six or seven months there, feeding on all kinds of fish. Some observers call them the "winged whale" because of the pair of long, white flippers that are about 15 feet from body to tip, the longest flippers of any of the whales. These humpbacks average 40 feet and have a reputation of being very playful. They may travel alone or swim with as many as ten companions.

Humpbacks sometimes have white on their tail flukes.

A humpback churns up the water.

Provincetown

The place where most of the East Coast whale watchers leave from is Provincetown, a small town on the tip of Cape Cod. Many years ago, men sailed out of this same harbor to look for whales, but then they were hunting whales for their oil and blubber. During whaling days Provincetown was a whaling port. Those long-ago whalers traveled hundreds or thousands of miles to find whales. Present-day East Coast whale watchers travel only a few miles because they wait for the warm weather when the humpback whales come to them.

The beginnings of this annual rendezvous take place in late winter and early spring. Humpback whales winter in an area called Silver Bank some 60 miles off the coast of the Dominican Republic. In the waters of Silver Bank the males crash their tail flukes on the surface of the water in boisterous behavior. They also flail their long flippers, and occasionally draw blood in a battle with other males over the right to breed with a female humpback. Once the breeding is complete, the whales begin their trek north.

As the whales leave Silver Bank and head north they find fish. They do not linger in any one place but continue their migration. Most are heading for the North Atlantic. However, quite a few humpbacks do remain at Stellwagen Bank, and spend the spring, summer, and fall off the shores of Cape Cod. These whales are seen over and over again by the New England coastal whale watchers.

The whales that continue northward eventually arrive in waters off Nova Scotia or New Brunswick in Canada. Others continue across the Atlantic, ending up all the way to Iceland. Scientists who study whales estimate there are approximately 6,000 humpback whales that winter in the waters of the Dominican Republic and migrate northward to spend their summers all across the North Atlantic.

Whale-watch Boats

These meetings at Stellwagen Bank between land mammals and ocean mammals are well planned in advance by those who run whale-watch boats. In March the whale boats, that have been winter-stored in a boatyard, are hauled out of the water to have their bottoms painted. Their decks and railings and inside cabins are cleaned and brightened. The massive diesel engines are checked over and the names of the boats on the

Whale-watching boats get repainted.

name boards are painted anew. When the boats are out of water at the boatyard they appear much larger then when they are on the ocean. Anyone standing on the boatyard hardtop next to the boats will look up and see them the way a whale does—from a whale's-eye view. The boats, 100 feet long, usually carry 150 passengers, with some boats taking as many as 400. The smaller number is desirable as people on board will always have a clear view of the whales from two decks and no one will miss seeing a whale.

The Start of Whale Watching

Whale watching began on the eastern coast of the United States in 1975 when a Provincetown fisherman decided to find out if people would be interested in paying money for a trip to the whale feeding grounds. For many years Captain Al Avellar saw whales while he operated his fishing boat out of Provincetown Harbor. And he knew that humpback and gray whale watching on the West Coast had been very popular for years. Often he wondered if people would be interested in going out with him to see whales. Summer after summer went by and Captain Avellar kept taking people out for a day of fishing. Finally, in April of 1975, he decided the time was right and he took out a class of students from Truro, a small town next to Provincetown. As soon as they left the harbor the students began seeing whales. Farther out they saw dozens of right whales. In fact, there were so many right whales Captain Avellar thought that finding whales to watch would be easy. For the next fifteen years and after thousands of whale trips no one has ever seen as many right whales all at once as they did on that very first trip.

Captain Avellar's fishing boat was called the Dolphin III. Later he had a boat built especially designed for whale watching. It was named the Dolphin IV. After that he had other Dolphin boats built—Dolphin V, Dolphin VI, and the Dolphin VII. Thus was the beginning of the Dolphin fleet of whale-watch boats that sail from mid-April to mid-October everyday of the week and several times a day.

When the success of Avellar's experiment became known, others decided they wanted to take people whale watching as well, and whale-

Whale-watch boats tied up in Provincetown

watch boats began to appear all around. In Provincetown three other whale-watch companies were born. Whale-watch boats also began sailing out of Barnstable Harbor on Cape Cod. Others left within sight of Plymouth Rock, the home of the Pilgrims. And boats started chugging to Stellwagen Bank from Boston and Cape Ann in Massachusetts. Maine sent boats to look for whales at Mount Desert Rock. And in the Canada Maritimes many whale-watch boats began taking passengers to see humpbacks, right whales, seals, porpoises, and dolphins.

Humpbacks are the whales that whale watchers enjoy the most because they are more gentle and friskier than other whales. They seem to be accustomed to the whale-watch boats and often swim over to be near the whale watchers on board. The whales may poke their heads out of the water and anyone on board can see the whales' eyes as the whales look at the whale watchers. The eyes seem so eery and mysterious that whale watchers may try to imagine if the whale is looking straight at them and perhaps thinking about them as much as they are think-

Humpbacks feeding

A humpback takes a deep dive.

ing about the whale. Many on board either stare in amazement or take pictures with their cameras. The whale, of course, doesn't announce when it will pop up its head or when it will decide to dive, so it is important to be ready because many a sensational photograph may be missed.

Sometimes the whales smack the water with their tail flukes, or they make noises through their blowholes similar to a tooting of a horn. No one knows who is having the most fun, the whale watchers or the humpback whales. When the wind is right and the boat is close enough, watchers can actually feel and smell the spout of a whale. The odor is a bit foul as it comes from the deep caverns of a whale's lungs. However, it is very thrilling to have been close enough to a whale to have smelled its breath.

Whale Adoption

About the same time the whales are heading north and the whale-watch boats are being readied, there is another spring ritual going on. Schoolteachers in various parts of the country are telling schoolchildren about whales. The pupils find out all about whales, how they are very huge creatures and that they live in the sea. The teachers use whale charts depicting different kinds of popular whales, and the students learn to recognize the various parts of a whale. They discover that the tail of a whale is called the tail fluke. They also learn that the long appendages on each side are called flippers. Soon they know that flippers have bones, but that tail flukes, which are 10 feet wide or more, consist of tendon and gristle. The muscular tail flukes on all whales are horizontal, which is just the opposite of a fish. A fish tail is vertical. Both marine animals use the tail for propulsion when swimming through the water.

Flippers have various lengths, depending on the kind of whale. The finback whale, that reaches lengths close to 90 feet, has short fins that are but a few feet long. And the minke whale has short fins, but with a white band across the middle, the only whale to have such markings.

A fifth grade class learns about whales.

Tail flukes are horizontal.

Humpback flipper

For some pupils it is difficult to understand that these huge animals that swim in water are mammals and not fish. Whales and dolphins breath air the same as any air-breathing land animal. Whales have some hair, they are warm-blooded, their young are born alive and feed on their mothers' milk.

The whales do not have gills for breathing like fish. Instead, they have a nostril called a blow-hole on the top of the head. (Some whales have paired blowholes.) When the whale surfaces it blows out old air and takes in a fresh batch of air. When it blows out the stale air there is a fine mist of blow-vapor or condensation that can eas-

Whale spout

ily be seen. Old-time whalers, men who hunted whales, used spyglasses and looked for the blows of the whales to find them. Often they would yell, "She blows!" and that meant that a whale spout had been spotted. Spotters on whale-watch boats do the same, only they use high-powered binoculars to hunt for the blow. Old-time whalers and experienced whale watchers can tell what kind of whale it is by the shape and height of the spout. Also, they can see if a whale has a dorsal fin on its back and where it is located and its shape. The finback has a small, sickle-shaped dorsal fin. The humpback has an irregular-shaped dorsal fin, and the right whale has no dorsal fin at all. There are also differences in the shape of whale snouts and tail flukes.

It is interesting to note that not all whales have teeth. The sperm whale is the biggest of the

Killer whale

toothed whales. A sperm whale has 25 teeth on each side of the lower jaw. The upper jaws have tooth sockets. The teeth are used for feeding on squid, their main food. Killer whales have huge teeth, with 10 to 13 on each side of their lower jaws. They eat sea mammals and fish.

The humpback, right whales, and finback whales, among others, are baleen whales. They have filters called baleen that hang down from the upper jaw. The baleen is used for straining and indeed looks very much like a strainer.

When the whale takes in a great mouthful of tiny fish and krill, it uses its tongue to squeeze out the water through the baleen before it swallows the food.

Once the students learn about whales and what exciting animals they are, they are told they can adopt a whale. When a class of students adopts a whale it doesn't mean they will have one swimming in a tank in the classroom. What it means is that for a fee they can learn all about the particular whale they have chosen.

A Classroom Adopts a Whale

A typical whale adoption took place one spring in a fifth grade classroom. The teacher handed out a sheet of paper to each student. On each sheet was a drawing of a humpback whale and beneath it were the given names of several whales with a brief description of each whale. There was also a whale chart taped to the blackboard listing many whales and showing pho-tographs of their tail flukes. Scientists who study whales take photographs of tail flukes because they have learned that there are no two tail flukes exactly alike. The tail flukes act like the fingerprints of a whale. They can be used to iden-tify a whale no matter where in the ocean it is spotted.

The students studied their sheets that listed the whales they could adopt. There were such whale names as Orbit, Silver, Othello, Blizzard, Fringe,

Students study the whale adoption list.

Humpback breaching

and Salt. Each name was given to a whale for some unusual identifying mark somewhere on the whale's body that whale spotters can usually see. Salt is mostly white beneath her flukes. Salt as a seasoning is white, so Salt seemed an appropriate name. Othello was named because his tail flukes had a large black "O" on the left side.

The students in the classroom considered many whales. Several hands went up when the teacher asked if they wanted to adopt Blizzard. Blizzard had much white on its dorsal fin, the small fin in the middle of its back. Others receiving votes were Orbit, Silver, and Salt. Silver was popular with the class because singer Judy Collins recorded a song about whales and Silver's own taped underwater whale song was on the record. Humpbacks are noted for the haunting and mysterious songs they sing, usually in the winter during the mating season. Silver was named after the famous pirate Long John Silver, who wore a wooden leg because he was missing his own leg. Silver did not lose a leg, but she did lose nearly all of her left flukes.

When the final tally was made the teacher said that Salt was the winner and the class went ahead and adopted her.

The teacher of the class also set a date to go on a whale-watch boat out of Provincetown on Cape Cod. When the students heard that, they were very excited. Most of them had never seen a real live whale. They checked the calendar and everyone said they could hardly wait for the day when they would pack a lunch and spend up to five hours at sea watching for whales.

Why Adopt?

Dozens of whales of various kinds are available for adoption. The reason for the adoption process is to provide funds for whale research centers around the country. The aim of these institutions is to learn all they can about whales, such as how they breed, where they spend their lives, at what age the females give birth to calves, and how best all the great whales can be protected. Whale scientists also aim to educate the public about whales. And most importantly they want to have strong international laws protecting all whales from whale hunters because the killing of whales is still going on in some parts of the sea.

For their adoption fee the students receive a certificate of adoption. They also receive a photograph of their whale plus a map to show the migration routes of whales. Whenever a whale is sighted, no matter where in the world, the

A whale-watch boat heads out.

information is recorded in a whale science center. When the adopted whale Salt is sighted the information is sent to the class. And if Salt has a calf, that information and maybe a photograph of the baby will be sent along too.

Fifth Grade Whale Watch

Finally the day arrived for the fifth grade class to go on their own whale watch. Everyone was so excited. First, they were going to see live whales, and do so by taking a ride on a whale boat. Also, they were going to miss an entire day of school and not be marked absent.

Early that day the galley of the whale boat was stocked up with hot dogs and hot dog rolls. There were soft drinks, a seasick medicine, film, brownies, blueberry muffins, and of course the fuel tanks were filled for the long trip. Besides the captain and galley gang there was another important member of the crew, a naturalist from the Center of Coastal Studies, a research institute in Provincetown. The job of the naturalist was to tell all the passengers on board all about the whales they might see.

When the fifth grade class arrived in Provincetown they were told some of the rules by their teacher. Do not run on board. Stay seated while the boat is running. Do not climb up on the benches. And most of all, no pushing or shoving.

Once the class was on board each boy and girl spent the time before sailing examining every part of the boat. They climbed the stairs or ladder to the top deck and then climbed down again to visit the cabin that seats all passengers. Some examined the rest rooms and others went topside again to peek in at the huge steering wheel where the captain sits when he pilots the boat.

Once the boat was underway, everyone was seated with their brown bag lunch at their side. Each young whale watcher had all kinds of sandwiches, fruit, potato chips, drinks, cakes, cookies, and some pies. After the boat left the harbor the naturalist invited everyone to the cabin to tell the class all about whales.

The students had learned a whole lot about whales in their own class, of course, but the naturalist narrated additional interesting facts. First she explained the safety rules of the whale boat. When that chore was over she held up a piece of baleen. It was the first time anyone in the class had seen real whalebone or baleen, and they were surprised to know it weighed a total of a ton in some whales. The students were al-

Whale watchers see a whale diving.

lowed to hold and feel it, thus finding out that the baleen was strong and flexible. Also the naturalist explained that the humpbacks they were about to see were part of a group of approximately 450 North Atlantic whales that are the most studied group of whales in the world. The naturalist held up a logbook and told everyone that during the trip she would be identifying the whales seen and logging entries in her book to add to scientific data.

The naturalist explained that because of everyday sightings, whale researchers learned years earlier that whales can be recognized. Once this technique was developed, scientists were able to gather information and keep records of individ-ual humpback whales during the spring, summer, and fall feeding time off the shores of Cape Cod.

As the years passed, researchers identified many humpbacks and gave them names. As the known whales had babies, the scientists kept track of the children and also the grandchildren of the whales. One thing the scientists found out was that younger whales returned to the same feeding grounds as their parents. Whales born to parents that feed near Cape Cod returned each summer. The same was true of whales that were born to whales feeding off Greenland or Nova Scotia.

The naturalist gave a few pointers to the young

Swimming whales

Blow vapor means a whale.

whale watchers. She said to look for the spout or blow-vapor water. She said it sprays several feet into the air. Once the students see a whale spout they should keep looking. Where there is one blow there will be others. There may be another spout from the same whale or from additional whales.

The naturalist said that the whale will blow perhaps a half dozen times during a series of short dives and then take a longer dive lasting up to five minutes. Only a small portion of the whale can be seen by watchers. Usually it is the back, blowhole, and tail flukes. The blowhole is located on the head. Often when a trained spot-ter sees just the back or tail it is enough to tell the difference between various kinds of whales. There is the position, size, and shape of the dorsal fin in the middle of the back. And each head, tail, and blow is different.

Also, students were told by the naturalist that they can tell when a whale will dive because they will see the tail flukes. If the tail flukes are raised high then it will be a deep or long dive. Sometimes the whale will be *spy-hopping*, meaning its head will be out of water in a vertical position. Scientists believe the whale is looking at the whale boats or whale watchers on board and perhaps trying to find out what is going on.

If they are lucky, the naturalist said, they may see a *head slap*, when the whale moves its body way out of the water and then slaps its head on the surface. Or they might see a *peduncle slap* when the tail is raised far out of the water and thrown down sideways on the water's surface or on top of another whale. The peduncle slap is considered to be aggressive whale behavior.

When the naturalist's talk was over, the students went outside to sit and wait. They joined dozens of other people eating lunch and gazing at the reflections of the sun dancing from wave to wave. After a run of 45 minutes the peacefulness was disturbed when the voice of the naturalist over the loudspeaker said, "We have humpbacks at two o'clock. There may be as many as two or three." Immediately most of the 150 passengers on board ran to the starboard rail.

The naturalist then said, "They have sounded—dived down suddenly. We'll wait a few minutes. Watch for their spouts."

BELOW: *Diving*   OPPOSITE: *Humpback about to head slap*

Within minutes the whales surfaced, a female with her baby, and another adult. The teacher and the parent chaperones warned the children not to get too excited. They didn't want anyone falling overboard and swimming with the whales. No one heard those comments because every girl and boy was staring openmouthed, pointing, or screaming in delight at seeing a massive whale.

Others were oohing and aahing. Some on board began snapping pictures, and a few had cameras that had telescopic lenses. All the children shouted at once as two of the whales, when noticing the whale-watch boat, swam over and started slapping their tail flukes on the water near the boat. The naturalist called that action a normal tail slap. One whale showed everyone its long, white flipper. That whale spouted and some of children were hit with the stale air. They all screamed and giggled and said that it smelled awful, but they were excited because they were close enough to a whale to feel its breath on their faces.

Up close the humpback was seen as sort of an ugly creature with its wide snout, chunky body, and long flippers. There were many knobs on its body where one or two bristly hairs grew, especially around its jaws, on top of its head, and on the flippers. When one of the whales dived the children saw how humpbacks got their name because the whale humped its back and showed its tail flukes before disappearing beneath the sea. The other two whales also dived.

The captain of the boat turned off the engines. The naturalist said they would stop and wait to see where the whales would surface again. Everyone waited, barely talking. There was no noise except for the wind and the waves splashing against the sides of the boat. Then, without warning, one of the whales broke the surface of the sea and flew straight up almost out of the water. The naturalist told everyone the whale was breaching and to look for the other whale. Not more than 30 yards from the boat at 11 o'clock the other 40-foot whale jumped almost out of the water. Everyone on board squealed and yelled with excitement.

After their leap the whales hit the water with a loud, white-water splash. Then the first adult whale breached again a little farther away. There were more screams and laughter. Cameras clicked, but there were also many people upset with themselves because they missed taking the pictures. As they waited there was another whoooosh and the second whale swept up and away, almost three-fourths of itself shooting out

Student whale watchers

of the water. Then the first whale breached again. Before the episode was over there were five breaches in all, and even the captain of the whale boat who had been on 3,000 trips was excited. It was a thrilling experience for the fifth-grade class.

Once the whales went back to normal activity, the naturalist told everyone that it was time to move farther along Stellwagen Bank. The cap-tain did not steer in a direct line. Instead, he went in a wide arc, probably knowing where other whales might be. Within minutes the naturalist told of a baby humpback at 11 o'clock that was on its back waving one of its long, white flippers. When the students heard that, they all ran to the port side to take a look.

There was a newborn humpback just a few months old waving one lonely flipper. It

Baby humpback slapping flippers on surface

smacked the water and everyone on board laughed. The baby's mother was nearby and occasionally surfaced. The naturalist said the baby whale was doing a *pec slap* or flipper-flop. The baby kept up the slapping, and the presence of the whale boat did not seem to bother mother or baby. After several minutes of watching the baby whale play, the skipper headed farther out.

Within a few minutes they saw a passing fin-back whale. The whale was like an express train scooting along at a good clip and not caring about the whale boat or the people on board. The students could see the difference in the back and spout of the finback whale compared to the humpbacks. Three more finbacks were seen from a distance and then the whale boat was steered toward home port. On the way back, one classmate asked the naturalist if she had seen their adopted whale called Salt. The naturalist said she had seen Salt a few days earlier and she was doing well. That information quickly spread around the boat and made everyone in the class very happy.

Back in port the class headed up the gangplank single file and assembled on MacMillan Wharf. They walked to their bus and on the way back to school all everyone talked about was whales. Many said they could hardly wait for a return trip to Provincetown.

Yankee Whaling

Many years ago children and their parents regarded whales in a totally different way. Instead of taking to ships to see and admire whales as done by the fifth grade class, people took to the sea to hunt and kill whales. Those children of the late 1700s and early 1800s had fathers who were whaling men. The entire family thought of killing whales for oil as a way to survive.

When settlers arrived in New England and

Fifth graders spot a whale.

Humpbacks are the most numerous whales seen off Cape Cod.

Cape Cod, they too found stranded whales and treated them as a wonderful gift from the sea. Even the Pilgrims aboard the *Mayflower* were watching whales. When they first arrived inside Cape Cod Bay they saw many whales all around their ship. Knowing they would have food, heat, and light from whales was one of the reasons the Pilgrims decided to settle in the area. Plym-outh lies directly across Cape Cod Bay from Provincetown.

Provincetown was one of the early Yankee whaling ports. Ships first set sail from Cape Cod in 1726 and a few years after that whale boats began sailing from the Cape tip. In its heyday as many as 54 whaling vessels called Provincetown home.

Every whaling vessel that sailed the oceans of the world had at least one person aboard who was watching for whales. It was his job to scale the mast and sit high above the boat watching for spouts. When he saw a spout he notified the man on watch and the entire crew was alerted. Small boats were set over the side and each crew rowed after the whales with the harpooner perched up front ready to drive a harpoon into the whale.

Watching Whales from the Air

Whale watchers today also observe the mammoth mammals from the air. Pilots take off in small planes and are able to fly over vast distances to spot whales. With a single plane a very complete survey can be made of the population of whales in an area such as Cape Cod Bay and Stellwagen Bank. Whales are also tracked by blimp. In as short a time as several days, scientists can come up with an accurate count of whales. Knowing how many whales there are at a point in time adds to the valuable information gathered by whale researchers and whale watchers.

There is additional value to flying surveys that are funded mainly by whale adoption programs.

Those on board, besides counting whales, look to see if any of the Stellwagen whales are in trouble. It is not uncommon for a whale to get tangled in a buoy rope or fish net. When spotters see a whale in trouble they notify an experienced crew to try and release the whale. An example of a rescue occurred in the summer of 1990 when a crew from the Center of Coastal Studies in Provincetown was able to cut nets from the mouth and back of a 40-foot humpback named Mallard. The successful rescue was led by Dr. Charles "Stormy" Mayo, founder and director of research at the center. Mallard's freedom was the ninth such rescue mission led by Dr. Mayo that helped save a whale. The fact that Dr. Mayo was the leader adds more interest because his father and grandfather used to sail out of Provincetown to hunt whales. In a way, Dr. Mayo's ancestors used to kill Mallard's ancestors.

Winter of the Whales

There is an interesting modern-day whale story that had its beginnings with a whale-watch flight. One winter in the late 1980s an aerial survey was being made of whales. It was early December and the pilot and crew of the small

Diving whales display their tail flukes.

airplane flew low over the coast of Cape Cod. Below the plane were the deserted winter beaches that were sandy and smooth, raked clean by winter winds. Chilly winds crashed on shore. The crew, with serious expressions on their faces, strained their eyes as they looked for something they hoped they would not find. They were watching for whales, but the whales they were looking for would not be swimming.

When the plane reached Truro, the town just south of Provincetown, those aboard spotted something in the distance. From the sky, about a mile to the east, they could see a huge, dark-gray shape on the beach below. By the time they were close enough for their field glasses to be effective, they found what they were looking for. There was a long, white flipper, and they knew it was another dead humpback whale, the second humpback and third dead whale overall.

Of course, whales have always died from natural causes, and in the beginning there was no reason to be overly concerned. However, within days, more whales were found on the beaches, and whale scientists, studying the dead whales, desperately wanted to know what killed them.

As more and more dead humpbacks washed ashore, researchers began to recognize the whales. Some were old friends to scientists, whale watchers, and thousands of schoolchildren across the nation. Some had been in the whale adoption program. It was a terrible feeling as day after day researchers had to log in another death.

One was Talon, well known to whale watchers out of Provincetown. Talon was the first whale that gave scientists proof that tail fluke patterns being used for identification change over a period of time, as some had believed. Found on the beach at Truro was Point, a very popular female. She, too, was part of the whale adoption program, and had had her second calf.

Whale-watching scientists and whale watchers everywhere were heartbroken to read day-by-day accounts of more whale deaths. As the dead whales were found, scientists cut out samples of tissue so that they could perform autopsies on the mammals to find out what killed them. Tissue samples were taken back to laboratories and then put through all kinds of tests. Schoolchildren who had lost good friends waited anxiously to learn the results, as did whale lovers all around the world.

All told, fifteen humpback whales died during the period of December, 1987, to January, 1988.

Scientists take tissue samples.

And the team of scientists who examined the tissues learned that the whales died from poisoning. Some of the whales had been feeding on mackerel prior to or on their way to the breeding grounds in the waters of the Dominican Republic. The poison is a naturally occurring toxin called *saxitoxin* that accumulated in the livers of the mackerel. When the whales fed on the fish, the toxin accumulated in their bodies and killed them. Scientists commonly refer to it as "red tide" algae. Its occurrence often causes federal, state, and local authorities to close down fishing areas until, through time, they are naturally cleaned up.

Despite being so disappointed, schoolchildren adopted other whales. The next year whales continued to travel north and the whale-watch boats, loaded with schoolchildren, adults, scientists, photographers, naturalists, and whale lovers of all kinds, saw familiar humpbacks again. The lost whales were missed, but others took their places and people keep going out to marvel at the size and grace of the giant mammals of the sea.

Privileged People

Whale watchers probably never think that whales at one time were land animals and used to have legs. The watchers are too busy making sure their eyes sweep in as much of the whale as they can. And the watchers may not realize that they are very privileged people. As far as anyone knows, whale watching from boats will continue for the time being. There is a beneficial blend for whale study institutions and whale-watch companies. The daily trips allow scientists to get to the whales to observe, and in turn the whale-watch boat operators pay the scientists to educate their passengers. However, other whale scientists are beginning to feel that watched whales are being disturbed by the boats that crowd their waters day after day. The whale scientists say that the whales are under stress. Therefore, there could be a day when the whale-watch boats are restricted and few people will be able to get close enough to a whale to see its magnificence and grace and feel its smelly breath on their faces.

Whale watchers are fortunate people.

Although the preceding concentrates on the Stellwagen Bank humpback whales, there are other groups of whales that are watched, studied, protected, counted, and adopted.

Gray Whale Observations

Along the western shores of the United States the annual migration of gray whales is observed by thousands. These whales leave the Arctic waters such as the Bering Sea and head to the warm waters of the coast of Mexico. The whales start south during November and pass close to the coast until they reach the lagoons of Baja California, Mexico. There they breed and give birth. The journey is 6,000 miles one way, 12,000 round trip, and is the longest migration known for any mammal. Whale-watch boats leave from ports all along the Pacific coast. Also, because the whales pass so close to shore they can be seen from land as well. Some shore restaurants along the

way provide binoculars to diners during the whale-watching season so people can watch whales as they enjoy the meal.

Killer Whale Watching

Killer whales are studied and watched on the coasts of the state of Washington and British Columbia in Canada. They can be seen by boats or from shore at Lime Kiln State Whale Watching Park on San Juan Island in the northwest corner of the state. In one year the killer whales were sighted by whale watchers in the park 154 out of 214 days from April to October.

Killer whales, or orcas, can be adopted. There is the Orca Adoption Program for orcas seen in the waters of Puget Sound and southern Vancouver Island. Up for adoption are any of the more than 80 animals that travel in families called pods.

Individual orcas are identified by the composition

A breaching humpback leaps out of the water.

and shape of the dorsal fin and saddle patch. They have such names as Sealth, Victoria, and Dylan. Sealth, the oldest bull, was first photographed in 1967. Dylan, a young adult male, was named because it is young and restless.

Right Whale Watching

There are few right whales in the world and they are considered to be the most endangered of all the large whales. Estimates put the numbers at 250–300 right whales in the western North Atlantic and approximately 300 in the northern Pacific. Whale watchers who see a right whale consider themselves very lucky.

Whale Adoption

If anyone wishes to experience the thrill of adopting a whale there are several groups offering various kinds of whales:

To adopt a humpback whale write to:

Whale Adoption Project
P.O. Box 388
North Falmouth, MA 02556   COST $15

Pacific Whale Foundation
Kealia Beach Plaza, Suite #21
101 North Kihei Road
Kihei, Maui, HI 96753   COST $15

Adopt a Fundy Whale
BIOS Brier Island Ocean Study
Westport, Digby County
Nova Scotia, Canada B0V 1H0   COST $25

To adopt a killer whale (orca) write to:

Orca Adoption Program
P.O. Box 945
Friday Harbor, Washington 98250   COST $20

To adopt a finback whale write to:

The Finback Catalogue
College of the Atlantic
Bar Harbor, Maine 04609   COST $30

To adopt a right whale write to:

Right Whale Program
New England Aquarium
Central Wharf
Boston, MA 02110   COST $45

INDEX